ALMOST NAKED ANIMALS™

THE DUCK VINCI CODE AND OTHER TALES

by Kate Howard

SCHOLASTIC INC.

ISBN 978-0-545-49291-1

12 11 10 9 8 7 6 5 4 3 2 1   13 14 15 16 17/0

Printed in the U.S.A.   40

First printing, January 2013

CHAPTER 1

"**D**on't you just love luaus?" Howie the dog sighed. "It's all about getting back to nature." He slurped his fruity drink and collapsed into a chair in the Banana Cabana's lounge.

Bunny — the hotel's short-fused activities director — looked miserable. "Too bad it's not sunny."

"Hey!" Howie cried. "That's a great idea!" He ran over to the wall and plugged in a bunch of huge movie-set lights.

Hisssss.

The outlet sizzled like an electric

pineapple roaster. The lights in the hotel dimmed. But Howie didn't seem to notice. He could almost imagine he was lying beside the hotel's super-de-dooper pool, soaking in the sun, resting up for his next big adventure!

Bunny hopped over and stared at the overloaded outlet. "Careful, Howie. You don't want to overheat the electrical system."

"You're right! Let's plug in a bunch of fans to keep it cool." Howie plugged dozens of buzzing fans into the wall, right next to the movie-set lights. He jammed plug after plug into the crowded outlet.

A minute later . . . *fizz*. The hotel went dark. The electrical system had shorted out.

"Oh, come on!" Howie moaned. "Hey, Duck! Can you fix it?"

The Banana Cabana's kooky handy-animal waddled over with his toolbox. "Okey-donkey," he quacked.

Duck opened his toolbox and held out his wing like a surgeon.

"Pliers!"

"Hammer!"

"Clamp!"

"Pineapple wrap!"

"Screwdriver!"

Howie handed over each and every tool Duck needed. The outlet crackled and sparked dangerously as Duck poked at it.

"Uh, Duck?" Bunny said nervously.

"Be careful!" Octo moaned, his eight legs shaking. Anything even a little dangerous put Howie's best buddy on edge.

Duck stepped back and took a bite of his pineapple wrap. The wires stopped sizzling, and the power whirred on. Duck proudly held up his screwdriver. "Fixed!"

"Great job, Duck!" Howie cheered. "I knew that nothing bad could ever possibly in a million years ever go wrong!"

Zaaaa-aaaa-aaap! Lightning ripped through the window and zapped Duck. In seconds, he was cooked like a chicken (er, duck).

"*Duck!*" Howie screamed. "No!" He leaned over Duck's charred body and yelled, "Stay with me, buddy! You're going to be okay. Lightning never strikes twice in the same place — *aaahhh!*"

Zaaaaaap!

Howie's voice cut out as a second bolt of lightning crashed down and hit Duck — again!

"Oh, no!" Octo whimpered.

Duck lay twitching on the floor. He was blackened and extra crispy.

"Poor Duck!" Bunny said sadly.

Piggy looked at Duck. Then his eyes slowly trailed down to the floor. "Anyone want pineapple wrap?" Piggy asked. "No? Okay, Piggy eat."

At that moment, Duck jumped up. His eyes glowed white inside his crispy, creepy, charred skin.

Piggy threw the pineapple wrap into the air and ran away, screaming. Duck looked like a bagel that'd been stuck in the toaster *way* too long.

"Duck! You're okay!" Howie whooped.

"Bouncy landings make happy endings!" Duck said.

"Uh-*huh*," Howie said, slowly backing away.

He was a little weirded out. "Well . . . the important thing is, you're still alive."

Duck stared at the others. "Traveling rodents mean you harm," he announced.

"He sounds like a fortune cookie. Hey, Duck! What's my fortune?" Howie asked eagerly.

"Something you lost will soon turn up," said Duck, staring blankly at Howie.

"That reminds me," Howie said. "Has anybody seen my lollipop?" He spun in circles, searching. "Hey!" he shouted, pulling the lolly off the back of his grass skirt. "Duck's not

a fortune cookie, he's a full-on psychic!" He took a big lick.

"Happy news is on its way to you," Duck said, waddling over to Sloth.

Sloth — the Banana Cabana's slow-moving bellhop — looked outside. "Look! It stopped raining. And there's a rainbow," she cooed. "I *love* rainbows!"

Duck turned to Narwhal. "You will have a gold record," Duck announced.

Narwhal beamed and smiled at himself in a mirror. "Outta sight! Only the most talented and handsome singers win gold records, baby! The Narwhal's finally gettin' his due. *Shoo-bop-a-doo!*" He danced away, swinging his horn.

Bunny looked at Duck suspiciously.

Duck stood still, staring at nothing in particular.

Blink.

Blink.

Bunny pulled Howie aside. "There's

something weird about Duck," she whispered.

"Duck's not weird," Howie argued. "He's just psychic!"

Howie and Bunny turned to look at their friend. He had placed a roasted pineapple on his head like a hat. He spun around, dancing and singing to himself. He wiggled and jiggled, still charred to a crisp.

"Okay," Howie admitted with a shrug. "He's psychic *and* weird."

CHAPTER 2

A few hours later, Howie was whistling cheerfully as he headed for the lounge.

"'Scuse me," a large giraffe blurted, stopping him. "No one gets past this point, okay?"

"Who are you guys?" Howie asked. A hulking walrus was standing beside the giraffe.

"Mr. Narwhal's security detail. No fans allowed in," the walrus growled.

"Actually, I'm not a fan —"

The giraffe got in Howie's face. "You're not?"

The walrus loomed over Howie. "Sir, may I remind you of how much bigger I am than you, sir?"

Howie's eyes traveled up, then down. The two dudes were, indeed, both huge. "Well played, my excessively scaled friend. Well played."

A loud *crash* came from behind the guards, followed by a sharp *bang*! Narwhal was obviously having a bad day.

The giraffe and the walrus jogged in to check on their boss. Howie zipped after them.

As soon as they set foot inside the lounge, they had to duck to avoid the flying furniture. Narwhal was having a whale-size tantrum. Drums, cymbals, and even sheet music were raining from the stage.

"This is an outrage!" Narwhal screamed.

The giraffe looked worried. "We're here for you, Mr. Narwhal. What's up?"

Narwhal flung his fins into the air. "What's up?! What's *up*!" He howled and wailed like a baby beluga. "I requested spinach *poofs*! Not spinach *puffs*!" Narwhal pointed at his plate and sobbed. Then he flipped the plate of offending puffs onto the floor.

Howie and the guards looked at one another, confused.

"Narwhal, what's up with all the drama-type stuff?" Howie asked.

Narwhal's sobbing stopped as suddenly as it had started. "Well, Howie, Duck used his freaky psychic powers to gaze into the future and said that Narwhal's on track for a gold record, baby! Fame. Fortune. I could blow this lemonade stand anytime." Narwhal stopped to pout and preen. "So you better keep me happy!"

He slumped over the piano and pounded his head on the keys. A dismal note blasted. "No," Narwhal moaned. "That's not it." He dropped his head on the piano again, and a more melodic note rang out. "Yeah, that's better."

Howie pulled out a notebook and pen. "Okay, so how can we keep you happy, Narwhal?"

"I want a humongous TV, a swimming pool with a *jumbo* jellybean dispenser, and a gold-plated sandwich-maker that compliments me!" Narwhal cried.

"Anything for my favorite whale," Howie said, scribbling notes. "I'll get right on that." Then he backed away, eager to get out of the lounge while he still could.

"And someone better go get me some Fruity Noodles — pronto!" Narwhal called after him.

Howie hurried off to fill Narwhal's order at the Fruity Noodle Hut. But he stopped short when he spotted Octo furiously taping something to the outside of the Banana Cabana. "Uh, I think I might regret asking this, but what are you doing, Octo?"

Octo didn't turn around. He just kept taping. "Well, Duck told me my dreams would come true!" he replied.

"Uh-huh . . . ?" Howie said.

"And I have this recurring dream that the sky is falling."

"Right . . ."

Octo slapped on another piece of tape. "So I built a protective pillow that will save us when the sky does fall."

"Gotcha." Howie nodded. He looked up at the padding that Octo had taped all over the hotel, then tried to inch away. But he wasn't going anywhere.

"Oh," Octo said. "Sorry, Howie."

Howie was taped to the outside of the hotel. "Well, I was right." He sighed. "I *do* regret asking."

As soon as he was unstuck, Howie strolled into the hotel lobby. He was deep in thought — about snot bubbles, and how he could assemble a cannon that would have enough power to shoot him and his friends to the moon, and also about how everyone was acting a little strangely.

"Gee, Howie, what's on that beautiful mind of yours?" Sloth asked dreamily. Then she blushed and quickly added, "I mean, what's up?"

"Ah, Narwhal's being a diva, and Octo's acting bananas."

"And . . . that's different from any other day because . . . ?"

Howie shrugged. "I see your point. But Duck's new powers are causing a lot of trouble."

No sooner had the words left Howie's lips

than Duck waddled over with a slice of cake on a fork.

"Oh, hey," said Howie, watching Duck nervously. "How you feeling, buddy?"

"Someone angry this way comes," Duck said calmly. Then he jabbed the slice of cake into his beak and strolled away.

A second later, Piggy stormed into the lobby. He was goose-cooking mad. "Who eat Piggy cake?!"

Piggy was so furious — and Howie so distracted — that no one noticed that someone was watching them. There was a spy in the Banana Cabana. . . .

CHAPTER 3

Sunlight shone onto Howie's smiling face. A huge framed photo of the heroic dog held a place of honor in the lobby of the Château Chattoo, the fancy hotel owned by his sister, Poodle.

A moment later, a tennis ball bounced off Howie's schnoz. Poodle was practicing her serve on her brother's portrait.

"Well, what did you find out?" she demanded, staring at her hench-animal, Batty.

He flipped through the pages of his notebook. "Well, let's see, Duck is psychic. And you don't want to try today's soup." Batty shivered as he thought about what he'd seen in the Banana Cabana's kitchen: Piggy sneezing into a huge cauldron of gumbo surprise.

"Really?" Poodle cried happily. Her automatic ball launcher shot another tennis ball her way, and she smacked it into Howie's portrait again. "That's too good to be true."

"Yes, he has seasonal allergies."

Poodle wondered if Batty had sneezed out some of his brain cells. "Not that part! I mean, having a psychic in my control will finally let me take over Howie's shabby hotel!" Poodle rubbed her paws together. "Batty, grab our disguises. We're about to get ourselves a psychic sidekick." She tipped her head back and laughed evilly.

Thwoomp.

A tennis ball hit Poodle squarely on the noggin.

Batty stifled a giggle. "I wonder if Duck knew that would happen."

An hour later, Poodle and Batty strolled into the Banana Cabana's lobby. They were disguised in mustaches and silly hats.

"*Allo?*" Batty said in a terrible French accent. "My wife and I would like to stay for

one night, *seal voo play.*"

Howie ran over to greet them. "Wait a sec . . . you look familiar."

Just then, Batty's mustache fell off. Poodle quickly slapped it back on his face.

But she missed: Now Batty had one giant eyebrow instead of a 'stache.

"*Non, non, non,* of course not. We are *for-ee-nors,*" Poodle said.

Howie shook his head. "No, no, I never forget a face, and I can see through any disguise." He narrowed his eyes at them. "I knew it! You're figure-skating champions Legros and Lagaffe!"

"Um . . . okay," Batty muttered.

Poodle clapped. "Yes! *Eet is uz,* but don't tell. We are incognito!"

"Yes, you *are* kinda neato!" Howie cried, winking at his two new guests. "Let me call Duck to show you around the —"

Before he could finish, Duck appeared at his side. "A summoned waterfowl will lead the way," he announced.

Poodle turned to Batty and whispered, "Look at that. Duck *is* psychic! All right, Batty, just follow my lead."

She flounced after Duck. Batty stumbled along behind her.

As Duck led them into the lounge, Poodle spotted Narwhal and Piggy. "Quick, Batty, get over there and create a diversion! I'll take care of Duck."

Batty hopped onto a table and launched into an old-school tap-dance routine. "Hey! Look at this!" he called to Piggy and Narwhal.

Narwhal and Piggy turned to watch as he cavorted and capered and did the cha-cha.

"Nice!"

"All right!"

Poodle was finally alone with Duck. "Thanks," she said. "The service was excellent. Let me give you a tip."

Duck smiled and put out his wing expectantly.

Poodle pulled out a net and threw it over Duck. *Swoop!* He was trapped!

"Here's the tip," Poodle cackled. "Never trust a poodle with a mustache!" She flung the net and Duck over her shoulder and headed for the door.

Confused, Duck peeked through the holes of the net. "This ghost costume has holes in it."

Batty stopped dancing and ran after Poodle. "Bye!"

Narwhal glanced at Piggy. "The little guy was pretty good!"

Piggy shrugged. "Yes, but finale need more work."

CHAPTER 4

A few hours later, the phone in the lobby rang. Howie grabbed it. "Everyone's bananas at the Banana Cabana! Howie speaking!"

"Hey, Howie," said Duck.

"Duck! Buddy! How are you?"

"I am at the Château Chattoo," Duck said. "Poodle is holding me hostage. How are you?"

"Well, I've got this recurring itch that's —"

Duck interrupted. "Bye, Howie. I have to go back to being a hostage now." He hung up.

Howie stared at the phone. "Duck? Hello?" But Duck was gone.

Howie looked at the rest of his friends. "All right, gang! Duck just called and gave me his latest freaky prediction. He said he's at the Château Chattoo, and Poodle is holding him hostage. Now, what can that mean? What is Duck trying to tell us?"

Everyone stared at him, trying to decipher Duck's latest prediction.

Silence.

Silence.

Silence.

Howie started pacing back and forth, thinking hard. "Poodle's a dog. She's my sister. She has pink hair. She owns a hotel. . . ."

"Oh! Maybe she's organizing a surprise party for me!" Narwhal suggested.

Howie nodded. "Fun! Nice! I like where you're going with this, Narwhal. Keep at it."

"Come on, guys," Narwhal urged his bodyguards. "Think for me!"

Giraffe and Walrus both stared into space. Suddenly, Giraffe giggled. "Heh, heh. That tickles! Thinking tickles my brain!"

Sloth looked from Howie to Narwhal, then from Narwhal back to Howie. "Guys, Poodle's holding Duck hostage," she said, frustrated. "*That's* the message. Do I have to draw you a picture?"

Howie and Narwhal stared at her, mouths agape, drooling.

"I guess so." Sloth sighed. Slowly, she started drawing a picture.

A few long minutes passed. Finally, Sloth finished her picture and shoved it in front of Howie. It showed a single white line. "There, you see?"

Somehow, Howie got it. "Duck's trapped at the Chattoo! To the rescue!" He raced for the door.

A moment passed, and then another. No one followed him.

Howie poked his head back into the lobby. "Guys? You comin'?"

Meanwhile, over at the Château Chattoo, Poodle was plotting her next move.

"Now that I have Psychic Duck in my clutches, the Cabana is as good as mine," Poodle cackled gleefully. "Batty, get room service to send up an extra-large chocolate pouffle. Tonight, we celebrate!"

Duck wandered around in his makeshift prison. "Noodles are tasty."

Poodle smiled. "Yes. Yes, they are! Tell me more."

"It is better to eat dessert than to wear it," Duck said.

"Well, that's not a prediction," Poodle complained. "That's just good advice. Tell me something useful, Psychic Duck!"

"Raining pasta makes bananas smushy," Duck said.

"Raining pasta smushes *bananas*, eh?" Poodle threw her arms up into the air, delighted. "Finally, some valuable information! Batty, raid the kitchen for noodles and ready the cannon. You know what this means."

"We're having a surprise party?" Batty asked cautiously. As he spoke, a mouse wheeled an enormous chocolate pouffle into the room.

Poodle stared at her useless hench-animal. "Remind me to fire you when this is all over."

Batty hung his head. "Again?"

CHAPTER 5

Half an hour later, Poodle was out on the Château's balcony, pacing angrily. "Batty! Where's the cannon?"

"You sold it to Cap'n Fizzy's Fuzzy Orange Summer Camp, remember?" Batty replied.

Poodle smirked, remembering the fun she'd had watching her cannon in action on all those innocent campers. Oh, the *destruction*! "That's right. Well, what else do we have?"

Batty wheeled out a catapult that looked like it was left over from a 1970s circus sideshow. He parked it next to Poodle's chocolate pouffle.

Poodle stared at the catapult, unimpressed.

"I found this in the basement!" Batty held up a handful of noodles and stuffed them into the catapult. "Oh! This thing even has a tape deck!"

La la la la la la la. Batty and Poodle relaxed as the sounds of soothing classical music filled the air.

"Oh," crooned Poodle, pleased. "That is good. . . ."

A sudden noise snapped her out of her reverie. "Now what is *that*?" She peered over the edge of the balcony. Her eyes bulged. Howie and the gang were advancing on her beachfront in a speedboat!

"Duck!" Howie cried. "We're coming for you!"

Poodle reached for her trusty megaphone.

"I'm warning you, Howie! Duck is mine. Stop your advance now, or I will unleash my noodles on you!"

Howie wasn't about to be stopped by a handful of overcooked noodles. His hero, Dirk Danger, would *never* be stopped by jiggly, wiggly pasta!

Howie pulled the boat up on shore. He, Octo, Piggy, Narwhal, Bunny, and Sloth hopped out.

"We'll never stop!" Howie cried, storming up the Chattoo's banks. Suddenly, he keeled over. He was pooped. "*Whoo.* Well, maybe I'll just stop to catch my breath."

Deep breath.

Gasp.

Gasp.

"*Okay, ready!*" Howie cried again. "*Never!* Duck is our buddy, and if you've gotta fire on us to get him back, well, bring it on, sister!"

Narwhal turned and fled. "I'll be on the boat."

"I warned you, Howie!" Poodle hollered. "Prepare to see my wrathiness!" She went straight to the catapult and prepared to fire.

Unbeknownst to Poodle, Duck had hopped into the pile of noodles. He nuzzled down into the squirmy mess like it was a nest. "Noodles are tasty."

"Batty! Fire!" Poodle screamed.

Batty did as he was told. The noodles — and Duck — zoomed through the air.

"Hang on, Duck!" Howie and the gang cried. They zipped back into their motorboat,

desperate to catch Duck before he plopped headfirst into the bay.

Duck and his noodles buzzed over the bay, straight toward the Banana Cabana. Duck giggled as he flew through the air.

Finally . . . *SLAM!*

Duck hit the side of the Banana Cabana! Luckily, it was still wrapped up in Octo's protective pillow dome. Howie, Octo, Bunny, Narwhal, and Piggy pulled up on shore just as Duck bounced to the ground.

"Bouncy landings make happy endings," Duck said.

"*Ohhhhh.*" Everyone sighed. Finally, Duck's psychic predictions made perfect sense.

CHAPTER 6

The next day, things were back to normal at the Banana Cabana. Well, as normal as they ever got.

"Howie-meister," said Narwhal, sidling into the lobby. "Sorry for flipping my lid the other day."

"No problemo, buddy!" said Howie. "Hey, what ever happened to your gold record?"

"Well . . ." Narwhal thought back to the day before. He'd been relaxing in the comfort of his new swimming pool, watching the tube and enjoying treats from his giant jellybean dispenser, when the TV anchor announced, "This just in! The price of gold has hit an all-time high. It's a gold record!"

Narwhal sighed. "Well, Howie, that didn't quite work out the way I planned. . . ."

Howie patted him on the shoulder. "It's cool, Narwhal. Hey, you know what's weird? Gold record? Bouncy landings?" He looked at Duck, who'd ambled into the lobby. "Hey, Duck, all your predictions came true!"

Duck stared back at him. "What is a 'prediction'?"

It was all happy landings over at the Banana Cabana, but things weren't quite as jolly at the Château Chattoo.

"Batty!" Poodle screeched. "How could you let this happen?"

Both Batty and Poodle were covered in

chocolate. The remains of the catapult were strewn around them. After they'd launched Duck and the noodles, the catapult had recoiled and smashed into the pouffle Poodle had ordered. Chocolate had rained down all over the place. The Château Chattoo was a wreck.

A room-service waiter strolled over. "Is the chocolate pouffle not to your satisfaction, madam?"

Batty swiped some of the chocolate mess from Poodle's face and tasted it. "Actually, it's pretty good!"

Poodle sobbed. Her perfect plan had been foiled!

"Hey, you know what's weird?" Batty mused, taking another taste of the messy pouffle. "Duck actually *did* predict that we would wear our dessert."

Batty and Poodle shared a look. "*Weeeeird . . .*"

HORN SWOGGLED

CHAPTER 1

"**S**hap dooba dibble! I said, whap wooba wibble!"

The crowd at the Banana Cabana went wild as Narwhal finished his set. "*I say, SHAP! WHAP! SNAP!* And that's the end, folks. You can go crazy now."

All the animals in the lounge roared with applause. Narwhal soaked it in. "You all keep it buttery," he said with a chuckle. With one deep, final bow, Narwhal trotted off the stage and into his dressing room.

"Another mega-mazing show, Narwhal!" Howie — the Banana Cabana's top dog — wrapped a towel around his pal's shoulders.

Narwhal beamed and used the towel to sweat-polish his precious horn. "I know, baby. My horn is tingling."

"Uh, should you see a doctor about that?" Howie asked.

"No, Howie, a tingling horn is good! Means my mojo is dialed to molto — *molto* as in maximundo *mojo*!" Narwhal finished sponging off. "Now, I'd love to let you bask in me for all eternity, Howie, but my fans are calling for more!" He headed back out for an encore.

As he bounded onto the stage, Narwhal chucked his soggy towel into the wings. It landed on Howie's head.

The music kicked in, and Narwhal rewarded the audience with some of his grooviest moves.

He chopped. "*Hi-ya!*"

He clapped. "*Ooh, ahh, ooh, eeh!*"

He kicked. "*Ooh, uhh, ooh ooh!*"

Narwhal's fins and tail spun and flapped as he sang, "*Everybody do the Tae-Kwon-Do-diddly-deep-do!*"

The audience grooved along with Narwhal. He had them in the palm of his flipper. They were *ooh*ing and *aah*ing over his every move.

"*Ooh ahh, eeh, yah, kaya! Chop bop a loo bop . . .*"

Narwhal finished his number with a triumphant leap into the air. And then . . .

WHAP!

Narwhal's head slammed into the ceiling. An instant later, **SMACK!** He

fell down and crashed into the drum kit.

The crowd gasped.

Narwhal popped right back up. "Ooh, it's okay! I'm fine!"

There was a moment of shocked silence. Then a lady-walrus shouted, "His *horn*! It's . . . *gone*!"

Narwhal laughed it off. "Don't be ridiculous. My horn is my everything. It can't be —" He

broke off and carefully reached one fin up to the top of his smooth head.

It was empty. Bald as a beluga, smooth as a dolphin, plain as a porpoise.

"— GONE! Aaaahhhhhh!"

With that, the always-cool lounge singer fainted.

CHAPTER 2

A few minutes later, Howie and the gang gathered outside Narwhal's dressing room. They were trying to coax their friend out of hiding.

"Did you find it yet?" Narwhal moaned from behind his closed door.

"We looked everywhere!" Bunny said. "On the stage . . ."

"In the ceiling," Octo added.

"In the alternate universe," Duck said. He unzipped his fanny pack, and a glowing, magical light shone out, casting a weird light over the room. Duck took a good look. "No. Not in here."

"Come on, Narwhal. Let me in," Howie urged.

"No way! No one can see me like this. I'm revolting! Unnatural! Freakish!" Narwhal sobbed.

Piggy shrugged. "So . . . no big change."

"But, Narwhal," Howie said encouragingly. "It's me — your favoritest buddy in the whole wide world!"

Narwhal grunted. "Go away, Norman!"

Howie blinked. "Uh, okay — your second-favoritest buddy in the whole wide world?"

"Not a chance, Leo!"

Howie looked uncertain. "Third?"

"Leave me alone, Chadwick!"

Howie kept trying. Many minutes passed. Finally . . .

"Uh . . . your forty-seventh favoritest buddy in the whole wide world?"

The door slowly swung open. "Oh, hey, Howie," Narwhal said sadly.

Howie stepped inside. It was pitch-black.

"Narwhal? Why are you sitting in the dark?" Howie flipped the light on.

Narwhal was at his dressing table, his head hidden behind a bouquet of flowers. "So nobody sees my shame-filled hornlessness! *I'm never showing my face again!* Such a waste of beautiful, blubbery beauty."

"You can't stay in here forever," Howie said, trying to peek through the bouquet.

"That's why I've ordered a specially designed shame helmet to hide my embarrassment." Narwhal shoved a magazine ad in front of Howie. A sad-looking critter

with a big log on its head stared out at him. "I can live off the mushrooms growing in the shower until it arrives."

"C'mon. Give me a peeky-see-loo," Howie pleaded.

Narwhal shook his head. The flowers shook with him. "No. You'll laugh, then cry, then perhaps throw up."

Howie put a paw on his chest. "I won't," he promised.

"All right," Narwhal agreed reluctantly. "Here goes."

He lowered the flowers to reveal his hornless head.

Howie stared. He tried to control himself. But it was impossible.

"*Hahahahahahahahaha!*" he laughed. He was practically falling on the floor, it was so funny.

Then the enormity of it hit him. "Boo hoo hoo hoo hoo!" Howie sobbed.

Finally, a wave of nausea swept over him.

He squeezed his paws against his mouth and choked out, "Excuse me a moment. *Uhn, oom, mmm . . .*"

Narwhal listened sadly to the sound of Howie throwing up. "I told you."

"Okay, so you were right. It is a *little* shocking," Howie admitted.

Narwhal threw the flowers to the floor. "A *little* shocking?! The horn is gone, Howie! The main of my mojo! The source of my scat! Gone! *Gone!* GONE!"

"*Pfft,*" Howie said. "As your forty-seventh-best buddy, I say you can sing just as well *without* it. Maybe even *better*!"

"Are you sure?" Narwhal asked hopefully.

"I *guarantee* it!" Then he whispered out of the side of his mouth, "A Howie guarantee is not guaranteed."

"What'd you say?" Narwhal asked, craning his hornless head to hear.

"Oh, nothing, nothing," Howie answered quickly.

CHAPTER 3

That night onstage, Narwhal flopped. He sounded worse than a wounded hippo. He moaned and wailed. His normally dulcet tones were completely out of tune.

The crowd stared at him in horror.

Booooooo!

Hisssssss!

Narwhal couldn't take it. He ran off the stage, sobbing.

Howie met him backstage. "Okay. So they miss the horn. But I have an idea!"

Narwhal perked up a little bit. "Are you sure it'll work this time?"

"Have I ever steered you wrong, buddy?" Howie said.

"Well, just a few minutes ago you told me that I could sing just as well without —"

Howie cut him off. He grabbed Narwhal by the flipper. "Let's go!"

A few minutes later, Narwhal returned to the stage. There was a plunger taped to his head. He scatted and bebopped with every ounce of mojo he could muster.

The crowd just studied their former hero

with disgust. It'd take more than a toilet tool to unclog Narwhal's mojo.

A janitor stormed onto the stage. "Hey, I'm gonna need my plunger back, buddy."

Narwhal tugged the plunger off his hornless head. *Schloop!* He handed it to the janitor. "You might want to wash that before you use it," he said sadly.

The next day, Octo, Bunny, Piggy, and Howie gathered in the lobby.

"Why are we here again?" Bunny asked impatiently. "I've got things to do."

"Narwhal told us he's going to make a big announcement," Octo explained.

"Tuskless-thing better hurry up!" Piggy grumbled. "Piggy has eye exam across town at 2:30. I go on number ninety-two bus that smell like old cabbage!"

Narwhal appeared at the top of the

stairs. "Ah! I can see you've all arrived for my very important announcement," he cried dramatically. "Good. I won't waste your time."

"Too late," Bunny mumbled.

"What was that?" Narwhal asked.

"Nothing," Bunny said sweetly.

Narwhal lounged across the banister and slowly slid down toward the lobby. "Due to my recent . . . um . . . incident, and the subsequent dip-diddly-depletion of my mojo, I have decided that I am" — Narwhal reached the bottom of the stairs and struck a pose — "*leaving show business*!"

"*Noooooooo!*" Howie gasped.

Bunny, Octo, and Piggy stared at him, waiting for more. But Narwhal appeared to be done.

Piggy shrugged. "Well, self-adoring fishy-thing will be missed. Piggy go now." He, Octo, and Bunny trotted off.

"I have to admit," Narwhal said, watching them leave. "I was expecting more. . . ."

"Narwhal, you can't give up show business. You *are* show business!" Howie cried.

"The old, *horned* Narwhal was show business, baby. From now on, I'll be the handy-animal around here."

"But Duck is the handy-animal," Howie pointed out.

Duck appeared out of nowhere. "I am Duck," he explained.

Narwhal draped his fin over Duck affectionately. "I have decided that Duck will be the lounge performer from now on."

"Duck?" asked Howie, stumped.

"I am Duck," Duck explained again.

"He's a natural. Look at those fierce eyes, hungry for the spotlight!" Narwhal continued.

Howie studied Duck. He stood still, staring off into space. A thin line of drool trailed

from his bill.

"I've made my decision, Howie," said Narwhal confidently. "Bring on the trouble. I can fix it!"

Howie nodded. "Okay then, handy-animal Narwhal. There's a light burned out on the back stairwell, the faucet in 241 is dripping, and the pool needs to be cleaned."

"Excellent! Now, if you'll just show me to my dressing room," Narwhal said grandly.

"The handy-animal doesn't have a dressing room," Howie said. "He has a shed."

"A shed." Narwhal grimaced. "How quaint."

CHAPTER 4

"Here we are!" Howie said cheerfully. Narwhal poked his head into Duck's shed and looked around uncertainly. "*Hmmmm.*" He poked around. His eyes finally settled on a cushy chair in the corner. Narwhal rubbed the chair and relaxed into it. It made a squelching sound as he got comfy. "I like this chair, baby. I love the fabric. Supple, cushiony, with an almost dewy feel."

"Duck calls that his booger chair," Howie told him.

Narwhal leaped up. "Sweet shiboobidy!" He flapped his fins. "That is *foul*!" He took

a few deep breaths. Then he grabbed a mop. "All right. I'll get to work now. Where should I start mopping?"

Howie perked up. "Ah, so I see you've found Duck's snot mop!"

"Oh, jumping jib-ah-dibby!" Narwhal threw the mop across the room. "Is everything in this shed made of mucus?!"

Howie glanced around the shed. He began to quake with fear as he realized that . . . yes, Narwhal might be onto something. "I . . . don't . . . know. . . ."

As Narwhal got ready to work, Howie returned to the dressing room to show Duck around. "And this is your dressing table. What do you think, Duck?"

"Where is the booger chair?"

"Well," Howie said, "as an entertainer, you can ask for any perks you want."

"Okay," Duck said, blinking slowly. "I want a sack of gravel."

Howie chuckled. "You can ask for a little more than that."

Duck blinked again. He thought. He thought some more. "Oh. Then a sack of gravel . . . and a small cup, also full of gravel."

"Oh-*kay*," Howie agreed. "Now, are you ready to go out there and entertain that audience?"

Duck paused to think again.

Blink.

Blink.

Think.

"I will need my hammer," he finally said. He headed toward the door to search for it.

Howie stopped him. "No, no, no. Why don't you just sing? Folks like singing."

"Okay," Duck agreed. "I am a good singer."

Blink.

Blink.

"Well?" Howie prompted.

"Where is my gravel?" Duck cried.

CHAPTER 5

That afternoon, Narwhal sashayed through the hotel, carrying a huge box of fresh lightbulbs. He stopped directly under a burned-out lightbulb at the top of the stairwell.

He stared at it, confused. "I'm new to this, but I'm going to go out on a limb and say . . . that's a lightbulb, baby."

He flicked the light switch. Nothing happened.

"Oh, come on. Are you *serious*?" Narwhal complained.

Flip on.

Flip off.

Flip on.

Nothing.

Narwhal put down the box and took out one fresh bulb. He held it toward the burned-out bulb on the ceiling. "I command you to change!" he cried, pointing at the dark bulb.

Nothing.

Narwhal jumped up and down, waving the new bulb at the old bulb. "This is impossible. Perhaps if I . . ."

Suddenly, he had a great idea. He tossed the new bulb at the old one. Both shattered into a zillion tiny pieces.

"Progress!" Narwhal cried happily.

But still, the light wouldn't turn on.

Narwhal stared at it, perplexed. Finally, another idea came to him.

"Aha!" He grabbed a stool and set it under the light. "Narwhal, baby, you're a genius." He climbed up on the stool with a fresh lightbulb in his hand.

He slipped.

He tripped.

"Sweet mother of kelp!" Narwhal screamed as he flailed and flapped, desperate to keep his balance. Panicking, he jabbed his fin into the empty light socket.

ZZZZZZZZZZZZZZ!

"*Yeaeeeaaw!*" Narwhal yowled as electricity coursed through his blubbery body. He fell off the stool and landed on the box of lightbulbs.

SMASHHHHHH!

"*Owwww!*" Narwhal cried. "Broken bulbs are *prickly!*"

He rolled down the stairs and smashed through the wall at the bottom. "Oobala. Ee. Oo. Wow. Oh!"

Narwhal pulled himself out of the hole in the wall. "Oops."

He looked around. No one noticed what he'd done.

"Howie? I made a new window." He brushed himself off. "Time for a break."

Meanwhile, in the lounge, Duck was making his debut performance onstage. Howie and Bunny stood at the edge of the stage as Duck — dressed in a fancy-schmancy bow tie and matching cummerbund — strolled into the spotlight. "Hello. Now I will sing. *Laaaaaaaaaaaaaaaaaa-aaaaaaa-aaaaaaa . . .*"

Howie and Bunny stared.

"*. . . aaaaaaaaaaaaaaaaaaa —*"

The audience stared.

"*. . . aaaaaaaaaaaaaaaa —*"

Duck sang on. Seconds turned to minutes, which turned into hours. Still Duck yowled into the microphone.

". . . *aaaaaaaaaaaaaaaaaaaaaaaah!*" He finished his note with a flourish. "That is all."

Duck glanced out into the audience. There was no one there. They'd all left hours ago.

"Uh, that was great, but —" Howie began.

"I think you're going to need to sing some *other* notes!" Bunny interrupted. "How about . . ." She went silent as the sound of someone screaming echoed from elsewhere in the hotel. "Yeah. Yeah! Just like that!"

Howie dashed off the stage. When someone was in danger, Howie was always ready for action! Though he wasn't always prepared to actually help. . . .

He rushed into the hotel lobby just as Narwhal appeared at the top of the stairs. Narwhal looked at Howie nervously. "Howie, so I — um — *fixed* that leaky faucet. Now, tell me. Have you ever thought of putting a water slide on the hotel grounds?"

"Why?" Howie asked.

"No reason!" Narwhal yelped. "Gotta go!"

Narwhal hurried out the front door.

WHOOSH!

A cascade of water erupted from the second floor. It gushed down the stairs and flooded the lobby, sweeping Howie up and under a huge wave.

WHOOSH! Howie washed up on the front desk. He watched as a family of squirrels rowed by in a suitcase.

"Keep paddling!" the squirrel dad commanded. "We're almost at the buffet!"

"Yay!" his kids cheered.

CHAPTER 6

As the day wore on, Duck continued perfecting his act. "Now I will play my favorite instrument — the musical saw!" He pulled a saw from behind his back and began to cut the floor.

The audience watched, baffled. This guy was no Narwhal, that was for sure.

Duck paused and looked at the audience. "This floor is out of tune."

Out in the Banana Cabana's courtyard, Narwhal was having an even harder time with his new gig. It was time to clean the pool.

"*Blub!*" He jumped in with a broom — and quickly sank under the water.

"*Burlb!*" he spluttered, coming up for air.

"Howie!" Narwhal gasped for air, then went under again. "*Splort!* Help me!"

Howie ran out to the pool. He stopped short at the sight of Narwhal, who was clutching a broom as he splashed and bobbed in the water. "Uh, Narwhal . . ." He pulled his friend to safety. "What's wrong?"

"I was trying to clean the pool, but I

can't hold my breath that long," Narwhal said.

"*Ohhhh . . .*" Howie said. "You're supposed to drain it first, Narwhal." Howie went over to the tap. He twisted the wheel, and the pool began to drain.

Narwhal sobbed and bobbed. "A real handy-animal would know that! I'm a *not-handy-animal*. A not-even-remotely-capable-of-semi-handy-animal-ness!"

An aardvark strolled across the pool deck. He stopped to gape at Narwhal. "Hey, aren't you Narwhal?"

Narwhal perked up and popped out of the pool. "*Yeesssss. . . .*"

"You were great!" the aardvark said. "When you still had a horn."

Crushed, Narwhal slumped back into the near-empty pool. "Yuh! I've lost my horn, I've lost my mojo, and I'm not even a groovy handy-animal!" He flopped and flailed in what remained of the pool water.

Howie jumped in next to him. "C'mon, buddy! You're Narwhal, the best at everything he does! You've just gotta get up and keep at it!"

Schlup!

A loud sucking sound echoed through the pool area. Howie glanced down at his pal, who had finally stopped flopping around in misery. In fact, Narwhal was lying completely still.

"Howie? I can't get up," Narwhal moaned.

"Sure you can! You've just got to stick with it."

"I _am_ stuck," Narwhal complained. His head was pressed tightly against the bottom of the pool. "I'm stuck in the drain."

Howie's eyes bugged out. The middle of Narwhal's forehead was stuck tight to the pool's drain hole. "Hang on, buddy!" He wrapped his arms around Narwhal's middle and began to pull.

"*Uggghhh! Ooougghh!*" Howie tugged with all his scrawny might. "Help me, Narwhal! Use your fins!"

"I'm trying, Howie. I'm a lover, not a struggler."

Suddenly, there was a loud *POP!* Narwhal's head was free. He and Howie sloshed and tumbled through the puddle-filled pool.

Narwhal stood up and shook his head to clear it.

Howie gasped. "*Whoaaaa . . .*"

"Oh, *now* what?!" Narwhal cried in exasperation.

"Your horn!" Howie exclaimed. "It's back!"

Narwhal reached his fin up to touch his head. And there it was. His magic mojo. His most-excellent, seriously super-de-dooper-de horn. "Really?! But how? Did horn fairies return it? Do they live in the drains?" Narwhal knelt down to yell into the pool drain. "Thank you, horn fairies!"

Kisssssss! Narwhal puckered up and smooched the sludgy, gunk-filled drain. He spit happily, then coughed out, "I love you!"

"Wow," Howie mused. "When you hit your

head, your horn must've gotten shoved into your brain!"

"Shoved into my brain?"

"Like this!" Howie slapped his paw onto Narwhal's horn. It disappeared back inside his head.

"No wonder I didn't feel anything!" Narwhal said dreamily.

"And then the suction from the drain pulled it out again!" Howie cheered. He squeezed Narwhal around the middle to pop the horn back out again.

Narwhal gasped. "It was in my head, Howie! It was in my head all along. My *mojo* is *BACK, baby!*"

Back in the lounge, Duck was still giving it his all.

"Now I will perform the classic 'Duck Stuck in a Box.'" He hopped into a cardboard

box and closed the lid. "Look. I am stuck."

Suddenly, Narwhal sauntered onstage. "*Hey now . . . !*" he crooned, pushing Duck and his box into the wings. "I'm a whale with a horn! The mojo is back, baby. Let's get buttery!"

The crowd cheered, relieved that the *real* entertainment was back. The lady-walrus cried, "I love you, Narwhal!"

"I love me, too, baby!" cried Narwhal, winking at her. He broke into a zoop-diddly-bop

73

performance. The audience cheered.

"It's great to see Narwhal back onstage," Howie told Bunny.

Bunny nodded. "Now everybody can just get back to doing what they're best at."

Back in his shed, Duck took off his bowtie and settled into the smooshy, nose-crafted comfort of his very own booger chair. He tipped a cupful of gravel into his mouth and chewed happily. "It is good to have things back to normal."

CHAPTER 7

"All right, gang!" Howie the dog hollered, dashing through the Banana Cabana Hotel. He was decked out in his most stellar beach attire: water wings, a snazzy snorkel, and ultra-stylish orange goggles. As hotel manager, he was officially declaring a day of sunny mayhem and underwater wedgies. "Who's ready for some salty, splashy, sandy, sunny fun?"

Howie sprinkled salt over his best friend, Octo. He doused Narwhal with a bucket of water. Then he grabbed Duck and shook him crazily in the air, grinning as sand sprinkled out of his shorts.

Howie threw his paws in the air and stared at his friends. They stared back.

Blink.

Blink.

Duck blink.

"Last one to the beach is a rotten —" Howie cried, racing outside. He stopped short and stared up at the dark sky. "— horrible, dark, windy, booger-freezing day?"

Lightning crashed. Rain poured from the dark sky.

Howie scurried back inside. "What's going on?" he moaned. "The sun's been gone for weeks now!"

Piggy — the hotel's chef — grumbled, "Piggy spend so much time inside, Piggy starting to go crazy as Duck-thing."

Duck stood nearby, chomping on a box of crayons. "Crayon?"

"Blue, please," Piggy said, shrugging. He took a big waxy bite.

"I've spent so much time inside that my tan is gone," Narwhal whined. He patted his precious horn and wiggled his pale blue body. "I'm as pale as a beluga."

Bunny sighed. "If the sun doesn't come back soon, they're gonna cancel the Rip-Roaring, Cotton-Candy-Cramming County Fair this weekend."

Howie sobbed and dropped to his knees. "Cancel the Rip-Roaring, Cotton-Candy-Cramming County Fair?" he wailed. "*That's it!* I'm taking matters into my own paws!" He shot his arms into the air like a superhero.

Ri-iiiiiiip! A loud tearing sound filled the air. Howie quickly covered his rear end.

"What are you going to do?" Octo asked excitedly.

Howie peeked down at his undies. "Well, I'm probably going to have to sew these shorts back together. But first, we're gonna come up with a plan!" He pointed at Duck. "Duck, go!"

"Okay. Bye, Howie!" Duck said. He started to waddle off.

Howie grabbed him. "No, Duck. I mean, what's your *idea*?"

"Simple," Duck said. "We should make our *own* sun."

Bunny rolled her eyes. "That's the dumbest —"

"— way of stating a *great* idea that I've ever heard!" Howie interrupted. "We'll make a *fake* sun! Let's get to work!"

Duck popped another crayon into his mouth. "I have a rainbow in my belly!"

Duck got to work. He picked up a hammer and began pounding. He took out a blowtorch and began blasting. He pulled out a sandwich and began eating.

As Duck worked and chewed, chewed and worked, Howie stood beside him, smiling proudly. *What could possibly go wrong?* Howie thought, giving Duck a big thumbs-up.

But Duck was the kind of guy who chewed crayons. So there was that.

CHAPTER 2

A short while later, the gang huddled together outside the hotel. The weather was still gloomy and horrible. Bunny, Narwhal, Octo, Piggy, and Sloth shivered as Howie and Duck began their presentation.

"Thank you all for coming out to this, the grand unveiling of the most magnificent and —" Howie began.

"Will you just get to the point already!" Bunny whined. "We're freezing!"

"All right, then!" Howie yelped. "What you've all been waiting for: sunlight!" He raised his paws in the air and punched a button on a remote control.

Ka-POW! The remote blew up in his face.

"And . . . I thought that might happen," said Duck. He handed Howie a second remote control, identical to the first.

Again, Howie lifted his paws and punched the button. A giant metal orb floated off the ground and popped up into the sky. It came to a stop just below a bunch of dark clouds.

"Wait for it. . . . *Waaaaaait* for it! NOW!"

Buzzzz! The metal orb lit up. It was as bright as the sun on a hot summer's day.

"Yay!" everyone cheered.

A moment later, it fizzled out.

"*Boooooooo!*" everyone cried.

Buzzzz! It lit up again.

"Yay!"

Fizz. It fizzled out again.

"Boo!"

Piggy stared up at the blinking fake sun. "Piggy freeze chops off for that?"

He and the others started to

head back inside. They were not impressed.

"Wait!" Howie shouted. "Duck, what happened?"

"What happened to what?" Duck looked at Howie blankly. Then he glanced up at the sun.

Suddenly, the metal orb snapped on again. Beautiful, bright sunlight beamed down on the Banana Cabana.

"We did it! We did it!" Howie cried, basking in the warm light. *"Let's Happy Dance!"* He grabbed Duck and they flailed around in a happy dance. "Happy dance! Happy dance! Happy, happy, happy dance!"

Several hours later, a crowd of animals in their undies had gathered on the front steps of the Banana Cabana.

The town's mayor, a trout, stood and greeted everyone. "It is with great gratitude that I award Howie and Archibald William Nightingale Duck the Third the prestigious order of prestige for bringing back the sun," he announced.

The entire town cheered as the mayor stuck medals to Howie's and Duck's chests.

"And," the mayor continued, "as a special treat, here are passes for the entire gang at the Banana Cabana . . . entitling them to skip any line at the Rip-Roaring, Cotton-Candy-Cramming County Fair!"

Howie gasped. "THANK YOU! THANK YOU! THANK YOU!" He planted a fat kiss square on the mayor's lips.

The mayor gasped and threw up in his mouth. *Dog lips!* He chugged a bottle of minty-fresh mouthwash. But the taste was still there. Like slobber, with a side dish of wet foot.

"Duck and Howie! Duck and Howie!" the Banana Cabana gang cried, pulling the heroes offstage and onto their shoulders. Bunny struggled to hold Howie up as they paraded around. She gazed up at him adoringly in the glow of the fake sunlight. "Howie, I am so happy! No matter what, I will never, ever get upset with you ever again."

CHAPTER 3

"Howie!" Bunny yowled, storming over to Howie. "I am so upset with you right now!"

Howie looked up from his perch on the Banana Cabana's front steps. How could anyone be upset? A few days had passed, and the sun was still shining brightly. It was perfect weather for blowing snot bubbles. Which is exactly what Howie was doing. "What's the matter, my favorite floppy-eared feline?"

"What's the matter?!" Bunny screeched. "First of all, a feline is a cat." She stared at Howie.

He stared back. *And?*

"Second of all, the fake sun's been blasting nonstop for three days!"

"I know." Howie blew another bubble. "Isn't it great?"

"No! It's horrible!" Bunny growled. "Now that the real sun's back, the heat is unbearable! And it's too bright to sleep!"

Howie ignored her. He opened a dictionary. "*Hmmmm* . . . what do you know? A feline *is* a cat."

"Howie!" called an angry voice. This time, it wasn't Bunny's.

Howie looked up from his book. The mayor was hustling toward them. Sweat oozed off his fishy scales. "What in tuna-tartare-town do you think you're doing? Why is your fake sun still on when the real one's back?"

"Ahem," Howie said, stalling. His friends surrounded him, looking hot and zombielike.

"We have hit a bit of a snag."

"I ate the OFF switch," Duck quacked. "I thought it was a crayon."

Bunny gaped at him. "So . . . you mean it can't be turned off?"

"*Noooo!*" Duck snickered.

"I don't understand why everyone's upset," Howie said. "I thought everyone wanted it to be sunny all the time."

The mayor flipped his fins angrily. "Not at night, you tail-chasing maroon! If it stays this unbearably hot and bright, the Rip-Roaring, Cotton-Candy-Cramming County Fair will have to be canceled."

"What?" Howie gasped. "No, you can't do that!"

"Well, find a way to turn off your sun, and I won't have to," the mayor declared. He started to hop away but then turned back and stuck his face in Howie's. "And by the way, if it's not turned off in the next twelve hours, I'm going to bulldoze the

Banana Cabana so that we can dig a big hole to store all the excess sweat our citizens have sweated because of your extra-sweaty sun!"

The mayor leaned back and took a deep breath. "So I suggest you get to work," he said calmly. Then he hurried off.

"No *sweat*, Mr. Mayor!" Howie grinned after him. "Get it? No *sweat*? Huh? Anybody?"

The gang glared at him.

"All right, how do we turn this sun off?" Howie asked.

"Howie," Octo said nervously. "I think —"

"No time to think, Octo! I've got a plan!" Howie raised his paw like a superhero.

Ri-iiiiiip!

"I'll get the sewing kit," Octo muttered.

Howie covered his bottom. "Thanks, bud."

CHAPTER 4

Later that day, the gang gathered in the lobby. They were all filthy, sweaty, and extremely crabby.

"All right, I'll admit it," Howie said reluctantly. "My idea of launching a garbage truck using a wooden leg made entirely of elastic bands may have been a mistake. . . ."

Everyone glanced over at Narwhal. He was wrapped in a full-body cast, tucked into a wheelchair, and covered in trash. A banana peel was draped across his head like a hat.

"You think?!" Narwhal snapped.

"Howie, maybe we should just —" Octo began.

"No time, Octo!" Howie interrupted him. "I've got another plan!" He raised his paw like a superhero. He waited. Then he peeked down at his shorts. Nothing. So he stretched his paw up even farther.

Ri-iiiiiip!

Howie grinned and covered his rear end. "That's better."

"All right," Howie said again. "Perhaps my idea of using a giant racquetball, a sledgehammer, and a marching band of fire ants may have *also* been a mistake."

He glanced sheepishly at Narwhal, Bunny, and Piggy. Now all three were wrapped in full-body casts and tucked into wheelchairs.

"Piggy very not happy with dog-thing," Piggy grunted.

"Come on, guys, use those things that help you think up stuff inside your heads. How do we shut this sun down?" Howie looked at Octo and Duck.

"Howie," Octo said. "Why don't we —"

Howie cut him off. "Wait, I've got another idea! All I need is an antigravity machine powered entirely by tomatoes!"

Octo and Duck looked at each other. Neither one was even the teensiest bit comfortable with this plan.

"Uhh . . ." Octo whimpered. "Howie, maybe there's a different way to turn off the sun." He sighed. "There *has* to be — because we're running out of bandages!"

A short while later, Howie and Octo trailed behind Duck as he searched through his shed. It was overflowing with strange, useless inventions that were piled on top of one another.

"Are you sure about this?" Howie asked Duck. "I still like my tomato idea."

Octo tripped along beside his best bud. "Let's just try turning off the sun from the inside first, and then we'll make your spaghetti sauce . . . I mean, idea."

Howie sighed. "Maybe you're right, Octo." He picked up a pencil and examined it curiously. "Hey, Duck — what's this?"

"A pencil," Duck said.

"A *pen-cell*? Can I borrow it?"

Duck nodded. "Certainly."

Howie reached back and used it to scratch his tush. "*Ahh!* That's better!"

Just then, Duck spotted something: a toilet with chomping teeth for a seat and lid. Then he spotted something even better just underneath it: a jet pack specially designed for three. Then he spotted something else:

an old pile of *Duck Weekly* magazines.
No . . . the jet pack was definitely what he
was looking for. "Bingo," Duck cried.

"Wow, great job, Duck," Howie said.

"Thank you."

Howie handed the pencil back to Duck,
who popped it into his mouth and gobbled it
down. "Delicious!"

CHAPTER 5

"When I said 'we' should turn the sun off from the inside, I was thinking more . . . 'you and Duck turn it off from the inside while I wait safely on the ground,'" Octo whimpered. Duck and Howie were strapping him into the jet pack out on the hotel's lawn.

"Don't worry, Octo!" Howie said happily. "There's nothing to be nervous about." He strapped himself in as Duck buckled in on Octo's other side. "Hit it, Duck!"

Duck punched the jet pack's START button.

Ka-POW! It exploded into a million pieces.

"And . . . I thought that might happen." Unperturbed, Duck led Octo and Howie over to another jet pack he had conveniently waiting behind the first.

Moments later, they were all strapped in again. Duck ignited the jet pack, and the three friends raced up into the sky.

"*Whaaaaaaaaa—!*" Howie, Duck, and Octo screamed as they soared toward the artificial sun.

"*—aaaaaaaah!*" Octo warbled on. And on. And on.

"Hey, Duck!" Howie yelled. "What does this button labeled DONUT PUSH do?" He jabbed at it.

The jet pack sped up. It shot this way and that. It zigged and zagged, totally out of control!

"*Whoooooooooa!*" Howie, Octo, and Duck screamed.

"Sorry," Howie cried. "I didn't mean to put my two bestest friends in totally awesome danger!"

"Aw, it's okay, Howie," Octo screamed back at him. "We all would've done the same thing." He shot Duck a terrified look. Octo was totally lying. He would never have done anything so crazy, ever.

The jet pack continued racing through the sky. A minute later, it had climbed so high it hovered directly above Duck's artificial sun.

Suddenly, the jet pack sputtered and spewed smoke.

"Abandon ship!" Howie yelped. He and Duck unbuckled.

Octo tried to do the same, but his belt was stuck. "Howie?" he said anxiously.

A second later, the jet pack ran out of gas and started plummeting back to Earth, taking Octo with it.

Howie and Duck didn't seem to notice that Octo was no longer with them. They were already falling toward the surface of the fake sun.

Howie landed first. Duck landed right on his shoulders.

"Oh, ha ha ha! Oh, oh, hot, hot potato, hot potato!" Howie yelped. His feet were burning up. The sun was covered in fire. Flames licked at his ankles.

Howie quickly hopped over to a metal hatch a few feet away. It popped open, and he and Duck jumped in.

"Cool," Howie mused, looking around. The sun hadn't looked very big from the outside, but inside it was enormous — like a giant spaceship.

"You are here," Howie read, studying a map on the wall. "Wow, there's even a frozen-yogurt place!" He pointed to the map. "Hey, Duck, can we stop and get some? Please, please, *please!*"

Duck squinted at Howie. "Only if you are good."

Outside, Octo was in free fall. The hard earth below was getting closer . . . and closer . . . and closer. . . .

"Howieeeeeee . . . ?" he cried.

SQUELCH!

Octo landed on the lawn in front of the Banana Cabana, leaving a giant crater in the ground. "Unhhhh," he groaned.

Just steps away, the mayor and his crew were ready to tear down the Banana Cabana.

"This way, boys," the mayor called, waving to a demolition crew behind him. "Who's ready to tear down this mess of a mess? We're destroying this dump in exactly" — he looked around — "anybody got the correct time?"

"Three fifty-two," Octo moaned from inside the crater.

"Thank you!" the mayor called back. "In exactly eight minutes!"

CHAPTER 6

Back inside the fake sun, Howie and Duck had been wandering through the halls for what felt like hours — though it was actually only a few minutes.

Howie was exhausted. "Are we there yet?"

"No," Duck said.

"How 'bout now?" Howie whined.

"No."

Howie grumbled as they turned a corner. "Now?"

Duck hopped over a giant red X on the floor. "Be sure to watch out for —"

But Howie wasn't paying attention. His feet landed squarely on the X. Flames shot out of the floor. Duck plowed into Howie and knocked him to safety.

"*Oof!*" Howie stared at the flames that had almost zapped him. "That was a close one!"

"I booby-trapped the sun so no one could turn it off," Duck explained.

"Great idea! Duck, watch this . . . it's like walking a tightrope." Howie was suddenly full of energy again. He dashed down the hallway. He bobbed and weaved as lasers shot past him and a swinging blade zipped past his head. He was like a superspy with

really bad breath and
really lucky timing.

Duck watched as Howie ran
through his maze of booby traps.
"You should avoid —" Duck began
to say. Just then, Howie stepped
on a giant button on the floor.
Duck pushed Howie out of the way
as flames shot into the air again. "Be very
careful," Duck said. "Watch every step you
take."

"Can do!" Howie cried happily. He
immediately stepped on another giant red X.

Screeeeeeeech!

The ceiling was moving toward them. They
were going to be squished!

"Oh," Howie said, staring up. "You said,
'Watch every step.' Sorry! I was still thinking
about the donut button. So, how do we stop
this thing?"

The ceiling was just inches away from
their heads now.

"With a simple code," Duck explained.

Howie tore an alarm keypad off the wall and handed it to Duck.

Duck stared at it, scratching his head.

"You forgot the code?!" Howie cried.

"What code?" Duck asked.

Duck and Howie crouched down. The hulking metal ceiling was coming closer and closer. . . .

"Come on, Duck, think!" Howie yelped. "Is the code your favorite color?"

Duck punched some letters into the keypad. "As-par-a-gus." The ceiling continued to sink toward them. "That was not it."

"Is it the name of your best friend?"

Duck punched it in. "D-u-c-k."

The ceiling was still creeping down. "No."

"Is it the street you grew up on?"

"Nose Nugget Boulevard —" Duck typed it in. "No."

"You know what's funny, Duck?" Howie said, glancing at the ceiling, which was now just

millimeters away from his nose. "I always knew it would end like this. This, or getting eaten by a giant mutant birthday cake."

"Of course!" Duck quacked. He typed in, "Giant . . . mutant . . . birthday . . . cake."

The ceiling came to a grinding halt. One second more, and it would have crushed them completely.

Duck licked the floor, relieved. "This icing is dirty."

Duck and Howie burst into the sun's central control room.

"We made it!" Howie shouted. "We're gonna save the hotel! *And* we get to go to the fair!"

Duck waddled over to the main computer

and started pushing buttons. "Self-destruct activated," a robotic voice announced.

"Nice work, Duck," Howie said proudly. "Now let's get out of here." He turned toward the door.

In a pleasant voice, the computer announced, "Self-destruct in . . . six seconds."

Howie stopped. "Six seconds? Did it say six seconds?" He stuck out his tongue. "We'll never get out of here in six seconds!"

"Self-destruct in . . . five seconds."

Howie stared at the computer. "*Five?!* That's even worse!" He paused, his happiness starting to fade. "Uh, Duck? I think I know where this is going."

Cheerfully, the computer said, "Four seconds."

"I knew it!" Howie yelled. "DUCK!"

CHAPTER 7

Back on land, outside the Banana Cabana, the mayor stood beside his bulldozers. The fake sun was still blazing overhead.

The mayor checked his watch. "All right, boys. Get ready. We're going to destroy that dump in—"

BOOM! High in the sky, Duck's sun exploded into hundreds of pieces.

The mayor looked up just as a giant chunk of the metal orb fell from the sky. It landed with a *thud*, crushing him and his bulldozers. "Oh," the squished mayor mumbled from under the rubble. "Oh, good, the sun is off now."

"Gee," Howie said the next day, "that looks like one fun fair."

Howie and the rest of the gang sat in wheelchairs at the edge of the county fair. Every single one of them was wrapped in a full-body cast. No one could move a muscle. They couldn't even pick their own noses.

"Quiet, dog-thing," Piggy grumbled.

"Too bad we're all injured and bandaged up right now." Howie sighed. "That cotton candy looks *reallllllllly deeeeeeelicious*!"

"Please stop," Bunny mumbled.

"Wow, those rides really look like a lot of fun," Howie continued. "And those games! Ring toss, target shooting, whack-a-moose! And look at the prizes!"

Octo groaned. "I don't think this could get any worse."

Suddenly, clouds appeared out of nowhere and covered the sun. Rain poured down on them.

"I was wrong." Octo sighed.

Howie just grinned. "Don't worry, gang. I had Duck install umbrellas in all our chairs. Just hit the red button next to your head!"

Bunny, Octo, Piggy, Narwhal, Duck, and Howie all stretched their tongues out of

their mouths to try to punch their umbrella
buttons. Slurp . . . reach . . . and *push.*

Ka-POW! The wheelchairs exploded.
The gang lay on the ground in a heap of
bandages and ashes.

Duck looked up from the mess. "And . . .
I thought that might happen."